Dog Says, Cat Says

written by **Marilyn Singer**   illustrated by **Sonia Sánchez**

Dial Books for Young Readers

It's morning! Do you have to go?
I'm bringing you my ball.

It's morning? Well, your bed's so soft,
I may not move at all.

Or you could take
me to the park and
we could run and run.

Perhaps I'll climb up on the sill
and get a little sun.

Breakfast first is fine with me.

Kibble in my dish.

Tuna, tuna, tuna, tuna.

Tuna, tuna fish.

Oh, well, I guess you have to go.
Oh, well, I guess I'll wait.

Oh, good, another bit of food
is underneath my plate.

Mailman's here. I must bark!
Stay away from us!

That guy never comes indoors. Why make such a fuss?

Look, a box! What's in there?
Let's open up and see!

You can have the stuff inside—
I claim this box for me.

What's that flying by my nose?
Wish that it would scram.

It's so buzzy.

It's so fuzzy.

Closer. Closer.

WHAM!

Come on, let's do something.
Let's have a wrestling match.

Go ahead and try it and you'll

see how well I scratch.

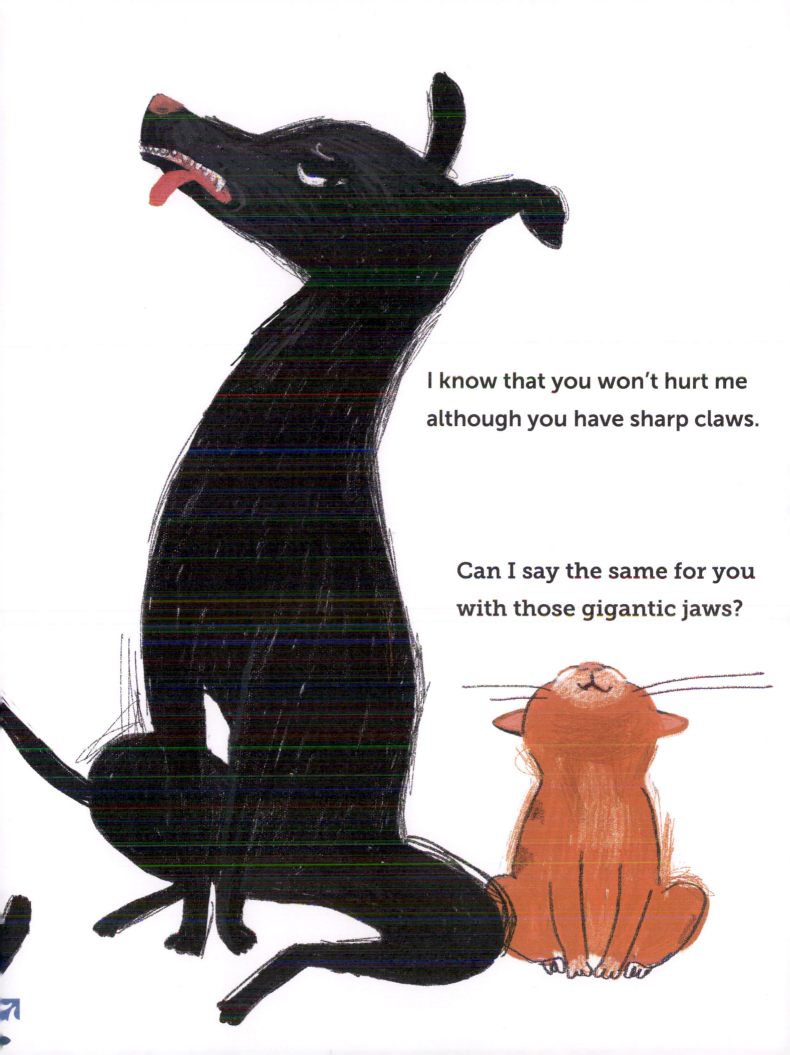

I know that you won't hurt me
although you have sharp claws.

Can I say the same for you
with those gigantic jaws?

I think, I'm sure it's almost time.
I'll go sit by the door.

I won't move that far, but I'll
keep watch here on the floor.

You're home, you're home.
I'm so, so glad.
I'll wag my tail to greet you.

I'd never wag my tail like that
unless I planned to eat you.

Come on, come on!

What should we do?

A walk, a run, a ride?

I believe we could hang out—
that's if we stay inside.

Hey, there's a new dog right next door! Maybe we can play.

There's a strange bird in the yard. Hiss, grrrowl. Go away!

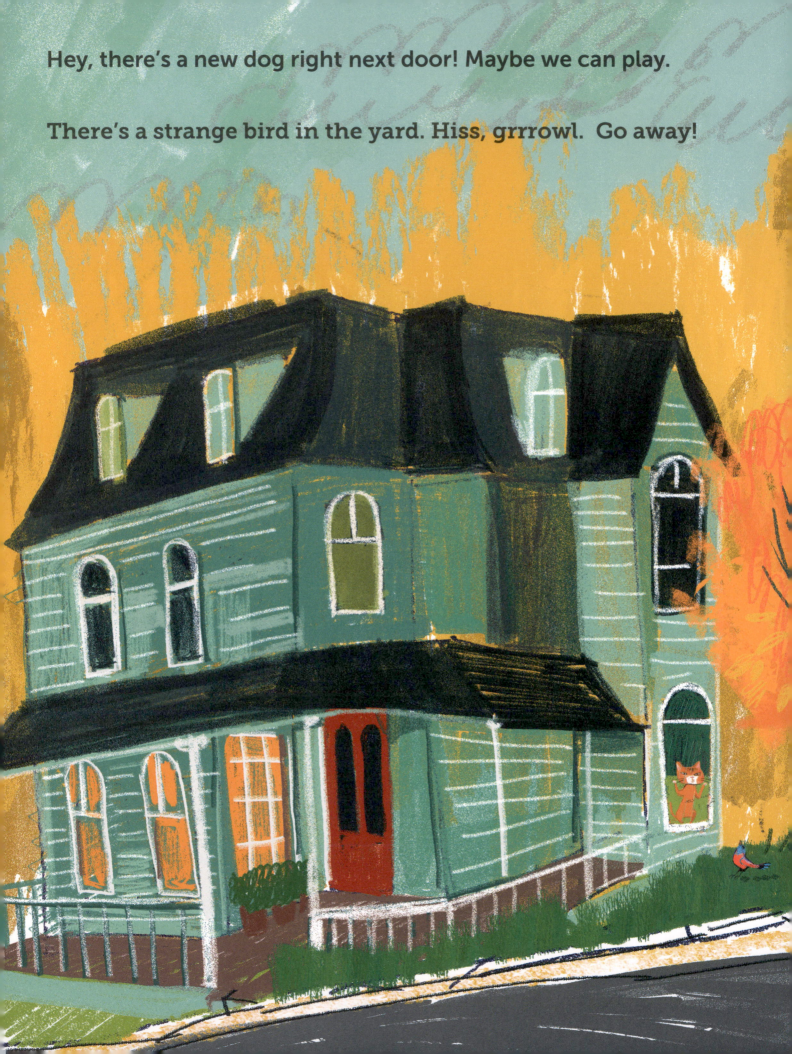

Throw it,

throw it,

throw that ball.

Tell me to go fetch!

I'll pounce and trounce
and leave it there,
then I'll take a stretch.

I just love it when you call.
I'll follow anywhere.

I hear your voice. Is that my name?
Well, I don't really care.

I don't mind getting muddy.
I won't need a bath, I hope.

You should learn to wash like me—
no water and no soap.

It feels nice when you pet me.
You are never rough.

Go ahead and pet me.
Okay, that's enough.

Yawn. It's time for sleeping.

My cushion's near your bed.

I'll stay up till it's almost dawn
and then sleep on your head.